Brianna
the Tooth Fairy

To Aleka Sumatpimolchai with lots of love

Special thanks to Rachel Elliot

No part of this publication may be reproduced, stored in a retrieval system, or transmitted in any form or by any means, electronic, mechanical, photocopying, recording, or otherwise, without written permission of the publisher. For information regarding permission, write to Rainbow Magic Limited, c/o HIT Entertainment, 830 South Greenville Avenue, Allen, TX 75002-3320.

ISBN 978-0-545-48494-7

Previously published as *Tamara the Tooth Fairy* by Orchard UK in 2012.

All rights reserved. Published by Scholastic Inc., 557 Broadway, New York, NY 10012, by arrangement with Rainbow Magic Limited.

12 11 10 9 8 7 6 5 4   15 16 17 18/0

Printed in the U.S.A.   40

First Scholastic printing, January 2013

Brianna
the Tooth Fairy

by Daisy Meadows

SCHOLASTIC INC.

The Fairyland Palace

Rachel's H[ouse]

Bedroom

Front Yard

Tippington Town

My tooth is aching once again.
But Ice Fairies shouldn't suffer pain!
I've thought it through, and now I'm sure —
Brianna has the only cure.

She makes our loose teeth a fun game,
So I've decided she's to blame.
Bring all her magic things to me,
And stop this toothy agony!

**Find the hidden letters in the star shapes
throughout this book. Unscramble all 10 letters
to spell a special word!**

The Moonstone Ring

Contents

Tooth Trouble

Rachel Walker opened her bedroom window and leaned out to gaze up at the starry sky. She took a deep breath of fresh air and smiled happily.

"This is going to be the best summer ever," she said.

Her best friend, Kirsty Tate, had arrived that morning to stay with her in

Tippington. Three long, sunny weeks stretched ahead of them. Rachel was excited to find out what adventures awaited. Whenever they were together, the most magical things seemed to happen!

She heard her bedroom door open and turned around. Kirsty came in, carrying something small in the palm of her hand.

"Rachel, guess what," she said. "My loose tooth has finally fallen out!"

"That's terrific!" said Rachel. "We can put it under

your pillow, so the Tooth Fairy can come tonight."

She closed the curtains and both girls changed into their pajamas. Then Kirsty slid her tooth under her pillow and patted it down happily.

"We've never met the Tooth Fairy, have we?" she asked, climbing under the covers. "I wonder what she's like."

Rachel and Kirsty had a very special secret. They were friends with lots of fairies and had visited Fairyland many times. Sometimes Jack Frost made trouble with his goblins. The girls had often helped the fairies foil his plans.

"Maybe we'll wake up when she comes to exchange your tooth for money," said Rachel. She got into bed and yawned.

"The Tooth Fairy is so quiet that she never wakes anyone up," said Kirsty.

Rachel smiled and turned out her bedside light. It had been a long day, and within a few minutes, both girls were fast asleep.

When Rachel's alarm went off in the morning, she sat up and looked eagerly over to where her best friend was sleeping.

"Kirsty, wake up!" she said. "Let's see what the Tooth Fairy brought you!"

Kirsty sat up and lifted her pillow. Then her shoulders slumped.

"My tooth is still here," she said, disappointed.

Rachel jumped out of bed and came over to sit with Kirsty. Sure enough, the little white tooth was still lying on the sheet.

"The Tooth Fairy is probably confused because you're staying here instead of at your house," she said, putting her arm around Kirsty. "I'm sure she'll come tonight."

"Maybe she left some money but forgot to take the tooth," said Kirsty. She picked up the pillow and shook it. "Or maybe the money got stuck inside the pillowcase?"

As she shook the pillow, the girls heard a faint tinkling noise. Suddenly, a tiny fairy came shooting out of the pillowcase. She did three somersaults in the air and landed on Kirsty's nightstand. She was wearing a ruffled skirt with funky red boots and a polka-dotted top. Her long golden hair curled over her shoulder.

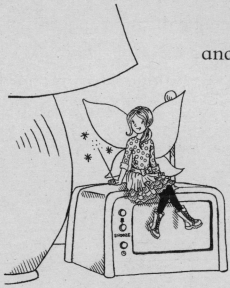

"Hello, Kirsty and Rachel!" she said. "I'm Brianna the Tooth Fairy." She smiled.

"Hi, Brianna," said Rachel. "Are you here to take Kirsty's tooth?"

"I wish I was," said Brianna, looking upset. "But Jack Frost has been causing trouble again. I've come to ask for your help."

"What happened?" asked Kirsty.

"I'll show you," said Brianna. She waved her wand at the mirror hanging on the wall, and the surface rippled. When it was smooth again, Rachel's bedroom had disappeared. Instead, the girls saw Jack Frost's scowling face in the reflection!

Scaredy-Jack

Jack Frost was sitting on his throne with a hand clamped to the side of his face. He moaned and groaned at the top of his lungs. Goblins scurried around his feet, cringing as he shouted.

"None of your silly cures work!" he roared. "I've tried rubbing garlic, potatoes, ice cubes, and pepper onto my gums, and

nothing helps!
My tooth still
hurts!"

He kicked
a tray that a
warty-nosed
goblin was
holding. A
toothbrush,
some floss, and a
tube of toothpaste flew
through the air. The goblin dropped to
his hands and knees to pick them up.

"Maybe you should go see the dentist,"
muttered the goblin.

The whole throne room went deadly
silent. Jack Frost sat up very straight. The
other goblins backed away.

"*What* did you say?" hissed Jack Frost.

The warty-nosed goblin looked around and realized that he was on his own. His bottom lip started to tremble.

"N-nothing," he babbled, scooping everything onto his tray and crawling out of Jack Frost's reach.

"I never want to hear the word 'dentist' in this room again!" screeched Jack Frost.

"But how are you going to get rid of your toothache without a den . . . um . . . without help?" asked the goblin.

Jack Frost snarled and banged his fist down on the arm of his throne. "If only I had the Tooth Fairy's magic — I bet my teeth would be perfect!"

Suddenly, a sly look came over his face.

"Goblins, come closer," he said. "I just had a fantastic idea. Only the Tooth Fairy's magical objects will stop my tooth from hurting. You know what that means, don't you?"

The goblins scratched their heads, looked at one another, and shrugged.

"You're going to steal them for me!" shouted Jack Frost.

The image on the mirror rippled again and then disappeared. Brianna turned back to the girls with a heavy sigh.

"That's exactly what happened," she said. "I sleep during the day and work at night. Yesterday, the goblins snuck into my cottage while I was asleep and took all three of my magical objects."

"That's awful," said Rachel. "You poor thing!"

"Without them, I can't do my job," Brianna continued.

"What are your magic items?" asked Kirsty.

Brianna used her wand to draw pictures in the air. The first picture showed a delicate, shining ring.

"The moonstone ring glows when it is close to loose teeth," she explained. "It guides me toward the children who need me."

The second picture showed a small coin with a star engraved on it.

"The endless coin allows me to put

money under every pillow. I can't collect loose teeth without it," said Brianna. "I put it under the pillow and wave my wand. Then the coin is magically sent back to my pocket along with the tooth, and money appears for the child to find in the morning."

The third picture was of a velvet drawstring pouch.

"I put the teeth I collect in the enchanted pouch. This keeps them safe until I can return to Fairyland," said Brianna. "Its magic helps dentists take care of everyone's teeth."

"Is there anything we can do to help you get your items back?" Kirsty asked.

"I hope so," said Brianna. "I came to ask for your help. Without the moonstone ring, I can't even find the kids who need me."

"So that's why you didn't collect Kirsty's tooth!" said Rachel.

Brianna nodded sadly. Just then, the girls heard Mrs. Walker calling them.

"Girls, time for breakfast!"

Brianna flew under a lock of Rachel's hair, and the girls went downstairs.

Mrs. Walker was carrying a pile of magazines out to the front hall.

"I've been getting rid of all my old magazines," she said. "I was wondering if you would take them down to the recycling bins in town for me after breakfast?"

"Of course we will, Mom," said Rachel.

The girls went into the kitchen and sat down at the breakfast table.

"After we've recycled the magazines, we can start searching for the moonstone ring," said Kirsty in a low voice. "We have to stop Jack Frost from ruining the Tooth Fairy's magic for kids all over the world!"

The Ring Leads the Way

After breakfast, Rachel and Kirsty got
dressed and put the magazines into two
large bags. Then they set off to walk into
town. It was early, so there weren't many
people around. The only people they saw
were three small boys wearing baseball
hats. One of them had a soccer ball
under his arm.

Brianna was hiding inside Kirsty's shirt pocket. She popped her head up as they walked past the library. "Girls, I can sense that my ring is very close," she said with a smile.

"I wonder where those boys are planning to play soccer," said Rachel thoughtfully. "They're walking in the opposite direction of the park."

The sun came out from behind a cloud and shone down on the three boys. Something sparkled on the tallest boy's finger, and Brianna yelled in excitement.

"That's my moonstone ring!" she said. "I'd know it anywhere."

"That means those boys are goblins," said Kirsty with a frown. "Let's follow them."

The goblins walked toward the center of town. They seemed to be arguing. The ring flashed brightly in the sunshine as the tallest goblin waved his arms around. The girls followed as close as they dared, hoping that the goblins wouldn't turn around.

At last, the goblins turned down a side street.

"Where are they going?" Rachel wondered.

The friends peered around the corner. The goblins had stopped outside Tippington Dental Care, and the girls could just hear

what they were saying.

"The ring's definitely telling us to go in here," said the tallest goblin. "It's gleaming so brightly I can hardly look at it."

"What if it's leading us to those pesky fairies?" said the second goblin, who was wearing sunglasses that were much too big for him.

"It's leading us to loose teeth, silly," said the third goblin in a very squeaky voice. "That's what Jack Frost said it does. He wants us to get to them before the Tooth Fairy does."

"Why?" asked the second goblin.

"Wake up!" screeched the tallest goblin. "Jack Frost needs as much tooth magic as possible, because his toothache still hasn't gotten any better."

"Of course he doesn't feel better," said Brianna in a low voice. "My objects aren't supposed to cure toothaches. They're charms that help dentists do their jobs!"

"Get out of my way," the second goblin said to the others.

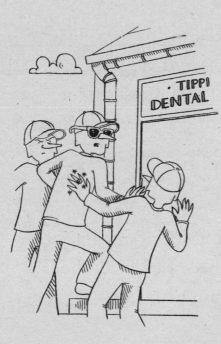

He elbowed them aside and ran up the steps into the dentist's office. The other two goblins followed, still arguing loudly. "Oh, no. They're definitely going to cause trouble in there," said Kirsty. "We have to stop them!"

"I need to get my ring back," said Brianna urgently, hopping from one foot to the other inside Kirsty's pocket. "We're so close — we can't let them get away!"

"We're *not* going to let them get away," said Rachel. "We have the perfect reason to go into the office."

She held up one of the bags of magazines that she was carrying.

"Of course!" Kirsty exclaimed. "Dentist's offices always need magazines for people to read while they wait."

"We can go in and donate the magazines and have a look around at the same time," said Rachel.

"Terrific idea!" Brianna cried. An excited golden fizz of fairy dust burst from her wand.

"Keep out of sight," Kirsty reminded her. "The receptionist can't see you."

Brianna ducked down again, and Rachel and Kirsty hurried up the steps and through the frosted glass doors. A stern-looking receptionist glared at them down the length of her nose.

"Do you have an appointment?" she boomed. "The dentist doesn't get in until ten, you know."

"No, we don't have an appointment," said Rachel politely. "But we have two bags of magazines we'd like to donate. Do you need some for the waiting area?"

The receptionist gave a flicker of a smile.

"That's very nice of you," she said.

"I'll go and put them out on the tables for you," said Kirsty quickly.

She took Rachel's bags and winked at her.

"Keep her talking," she whispered. "I'm going to find those goblins!"

The Great Goblin Tooth Hunt

Rachel stood in front of the receptionist's desk and blocked her view of the waiting area. Kirsty put the magazines on the table and then looked around. The door to the exam room was slightly open. She stepped closer and heard a muffled giggle coming from inside.

"That was a goblin!" Brianna whispered. "Let's investigate."

"OK," Kirsty replied in a low voice. "The dentist doesn't come in until ten. That gives us half an hour."

Kirsty glanced over at her best friend. Rachel was chatting with the receptionist about the Tippington summer carnival. Kirsty pushed open the door to the exam room and peeked inside.

CRASH! BANG! SPLASH! The goblins had turned the examination room into a disaster area. Cupboards had been thrown open and dental equipment was scattered on the floor. The tallest goblin sat in the exam chair and played with the mouthwash dispenser. The goblin with the squeaky voice giggled as he hung upside down.

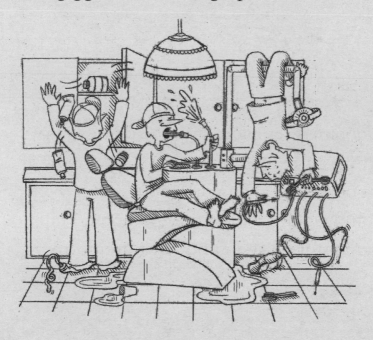

"Those troublemakers!" Kirsty exclaimed.

Brianna peeked out of Kirsty's shirt pocket and gasped. The goblin wearing  sunglasses had a mouthful of pink mouthwash and was spitting it at the others. As the girls watched, he sprayed the last drops over the squeaky-voiced goblin, then picked up the dentist's drill and started to make holes in the wall. The goblin, dripping with mouthwash, next jumped up to grab a low-hanging light, and started swinging back and forth.

"Can you see any teeth
from up there?"
demanded the tallest
goblin.
"Who cares —
this is fun!"
squealed
the other
goblin,
swinging
faster and faster.

"You'll care when Jack Frost catches
you!" said the tallest goblin, shining the
dentist's light into the eyes of the other
goblin.

"OW!" screeched the goblin. "Stop
it!" He let go of the light and crashed to
the floor.

"Hey, look at me!" said the goblin with the squeaky voice.

He filled a mold with pink dental wax and bit into it to make a copy of his teeth. But he couldn't pull it out of his mouth!

"OWWW!" he wailed.

The other goblins cackled with laughter, holding their stomachs and rolling around on the floor. The tallest goblin rolled into a cabinet, which burst open. A cascade of false teeth rained down on him.

"Get them!" he squawked.

The goblins lunged for the false teeth. They obviously thought they were real, and could help Jack Frost!

"We have to stop them!" cried Brianna. She zoomed out of Kirsty's pocket and into the exam room.

Kirsty followed her and stood with her back against the door.

"Stop!" she demanded. "Those don't belong to you. Put them back!"

"No way!" snapped the

tallest goblin. "These are for Jack Frost, not for silly humans and pesky fairies."

Kirsty had to think of a way to get Brianna's ring back. She winked at Brianna to show her that she had a plan.

"Jack Frost won't want boring old fake teeth like that," she said. "Brianna could use her magic to make you some that are much better. Don't you think Jack Frost would like special windup teeth that jump and chatter on their own?"

"That sounds great!" The goblin with sunglasses gasped.

"All you have to do is give us that ring

on your finger," said Kirsty, "and
Brianna will create three wonderful new
sets of windup teeth for you."

"What do you think, goblins? Does
that sound fair?" asked Brianna.

Gifts for the Goblins

The goblins looked at one another.

"I bet Jack Frost would be really happy with us if we brought him three whole sets of windup teeth," said the one with the squeaky voice.

"He won't care about the ring when he sees that we brought him such exciting teeth," the tallest goblin agreed.

They turned to Kirsty and Brianna, and nodded.

"It's a deal!" they said together.

Then the tallest goblin removed the ring and held it out. Brianna fluttered over to him and took it. Instantly, the ring shrank to fairy-size, and Brianna slipped it onto her finger.

"Now give us what you promised!" demanded the goblin with sunglasses.

Brianna waved her wand and said a spell.

"Chatter, natter, grind, and chew,
These goblins all want something new.
Give each one a set of teeth
To take back to their
    icy chief."

With a golden, sparkling flash, each goblin had a set of plastic windup teeth in his hand. They laughed and squawked with delight

as the teeth jumped
around and
chattered.

"Let's get
out of here
before those
tricky
humans try
to stop us!"
shouted the
goblin with the
sunglasses.

One by one, the goblins leaped out of
the open window and ran away.
Brianna cleaned up the exam room with
one swish of her wand. Then she darted
into Kirsty's pocket, and Kirsty walked
back out to the waiting area.

"All done," she called to Rachel, giving her a thumbs-up.

"Thank you for the magazines," said the receptionist.

Rachel and Kirsty hurried down the steps and hugged each other. Brianna popped out of Kirsty's pocket and wiggled her hand around in delight. The moonstone ring sparkled in the sunshine.

"You got the ring back!" Rachel exclaimed. "Good job!"

"Does this mean you can take my tooth now?" Kirsty asked.

"I'm sorry, Kirsty, but I can't," said Brianna. "I still need the endless coin and the enchanted pouch — and the goblins still have those."

"Then we'll just have to find them as fast as we can," said Rachel, giving her friend's hand a comforting squeeze.

"Put the tooth back under your pillow," Brianna told Kirsty. "You have both been so wonderful. I'm sure that with your help, we'll find the endless coin and the enchanted pouch very soon."

"We'll do our best!" said Kirsty.

"I have to return to Fairyland now," said Brianna, "but I'll be back as soon as I have any news."

As the moonstone ring gave a final flash, she twirled into the air and disappeared in a puff of golden fairy dust.

Rachel and Kirsty looked at each other and smiled.

"Let's go home and put that tooth back under your pillow," said Rachel. "I have a feeling that Brianna will be able to take it very, very soon!"

The Endless Coin

Contents

Things That Go Bump in the Night

Kirsty opened her eyes and blinked a few times. The bedroom was completely dark, and she could hear Rachel's steady breathing on the other side of the room. It was the middle of the night, and she wasn't sure what had woken her up.

She heard a soft rustling noise and felt

her pillow lift up slightly. Someone was in their room!

"Hey!" she exclaimed, sitting bolt upright.

There was a muffled squawk from beside her bed, and something bumped into the nightstand.

"What's the matter?" asked Rachel,
instantly awake.

Kirsty had
recognized
the squawk.

"Rachel,
I think a
goblin just
tried to steal
my tooth!"
she said.

Rachel gasped and switched on
her bedside lamp. The girls looked
around the room, but everything seemed
to be normal. There wasn't a goblin in
sight.

"Are you sure you weren't dreaming?"
askcd Rachel.

"I don't think so," said Kirsty.

She leaned over the side of the bed and peered into the darkness underneath. The light from the lamp was dim, so at first, she couldn't see anything. Then she spotted two greenish eyes glaring at her from the shadows.

"He's under here!" she cried.

Rachel jumped out of bed as the goblin scurried out of his hiding place. He dived for the door,

but his feet got tangled in the lamp cord. There was another yell and a crash, and

the light went out. The girls heard the
goblin groan. He had knocked the lamp
onto his bony head.

"Don't let him get away!" said Kirsty.
She got out of bed and felt around the
floor in the dark, trying to grab the
goblin's feet.

"I don't know where he went!" Rachel replied, stretching out her hands at goblin height.

"I found the lamp," said Kirsty, pressing the switch. "And it works!"

The room was flooded with light again, and the girls looked around. The goblin was nowhere to be seen.

"Let's check under the beds again," Rachel suggested.

They looked carefully, but the goblin wasn't hiding under the beds this time. Rachel pulled the curtain aside and noticed that the window was open.

"Maybe he climbed out the window and down the tree," she said. "Did he take your tooth?"

Kirsty felt under her pillow and smiled.

"No," she said, "it's still here."

Just then, the bedroom door opened and Mr. Walker's head appeared around it. He blinked sleepily.

"Are you girls all right?" he asked. "We heard a crash."

"Sorry, Dad," said Rachel, climbing back into bed. "The lamp got knocked over, but it's not broken."

"Well, turn out the light and go to sleep," Mr. Walker said. "It's the middle of the night, you know."

He went back to bed, and Rachel switched off the lamp. No one noticed that the wardrobe door was now slightly open. Kirsty and Rachel lay down and closed their eyes.

Buttons Barks a Warning!

The girls woke up late after their midnight adventure. They dressed quickly and hurried downstairs for breakfast. Mr. and Mrs. Walker had already eaten, and Mr. Walker was putting on his shoes to go to work.

"Morning, Dad," said Rachel, giving him a kiss on the cheek. "Sorry we woke you up last night."

"You must have been having a very exciting dream to knock your lamp over in your sleep!" he said with a laugh.

Rachel just smiled. She couldn't admit that it was really a goblin who had caused all that trouble. Her dad would never believe that a goblin had knocked over the lamp!

Just then, Rachel's dog, Buttons, started to bark upstairs.

"Quiet, Buttons!" called Mr. Walker.

He turned back to Rachel and Kirsty. "I have to leave for work now. Bye, girls!"

Rachel and Kirsty said good-bye and then went into the kitchen. Rachel poured some cereal, and Mrs. Walker went out into the backyard to hang up some laundry. As Kirsty reached for the cornflakes, the little white milk jug on the breakfast table began to glow. The girls knew immediately that something magical was about to happen!

A puff of golden fairy dust sparkled around the top of the jug.

Brianna the Tooth
Fairy popped out and
twirled in the air!
She landed softly on
the table in front of
Rachel, and a little
fairy dust sprinkled
onto the tablecloth.

"Good morning!"
she said in a bright
voice. "I've come to
tell you some news from
Fairyland."

"Have you found your other magical
objects?" asked Kirsty.

"Not yet," said Brianna. "But I have
an idea where they might be. Fern the
Green Fairy was visiting a tree near the
Ice Castle, and she overheard some goblins

talking. Jack Frost has sent one goblin to the human world with the endless coin. He's ordered him to pose as me and steal any teeth that children leave out for the Tooth Fairy."

Rachel gave a little gasp.

"Brianna, there was a goblin in our room last night," she said.

They explained what had happened in the middle of the night. The little fairy's eyes lit up with hope.

"If he was trying to take your tooth, he must have had the endless coin," she said. "It's impossible to take teeth from under pillows without it."

"Why does Jack Frost want the goblin to pretend to be the Tooth Fairy?" asked Kirsty.

"He wants to use my stolen objects to harness my Tooth Fairy magic," Brianna explained. "He thinks it will cure his toothache and protect him from getting one in the future."

Rachel opened her mouth to ask another question, but just then, Buttons started to

bark again. The girls exchanged a
worried glance.

"That's Buttons's warning bark," said
Rachel.

"Something must be wrong," Kirsty
exclaimed, quickly jumping to her feet.
"Come on!"

They raced up the stairs two at a time,
and Brianna flew above their heads.
Buttons was getting more frantic. He
gave a series of deep barks that echoed
through the whole house.

"He's in your bedroom, Rachel!" said Kirsty, racing into the room.

Buttons stood in front of the wardrobe, barking with all his might. All the hair on his neck was standing up.

"What's wrong, Buttons?" Rachel asked, putting her hand on the dog's soft head.

Buttons looked up at her and gave a little woof. Then he stared back at the wardrobe. The girls could now see that the door was slightly

open. They exchanged a worried look.
Rachel bravely stepped forward and
pulled the door wide open.

"EEEEEE!"

A squealing, wailing bundle fell out of
the wardrobe, rolled across the floor, and
landed at Rachel's feet!

The Bad-Tempered Bundle

The bundle jumped up, and the girls saw
that it had two spindly green legs, two
scrawny green arms, and a very bumpy
green head.

"It's a goblin!" cried Kirsty.

He didn't look like a normal goblin.
He was wearing three skirts, two dresses,

four pairs of pants, a knitted hat, and a cardigan sweater.

Rachel cried out in surprise. "He's wearing all my clothes from inside the wardrobe!" she exclaimed. "Take those off right now! They don't belong to you."

The goblin scowled at her.

"No," he said, sticking out his tongue out at her. "I'm not going to let that monster bite me! Its fangs will

never get through all these
protective layers."

"Buttons
isn't a
monster —
he's just
my pet
dog!" said
Rachel. "He
would never
bite anyone."

"I don't believe
you," replied the goblin. "Go away
and leave me alone. Take that monster
with you."

"You can't order Rachel around in her
own bedroom," said Brianna. "You're
the one who doesn't belong here."

"What are you going to do about it, you silly fairy?" the goblin demanded with a sneer. "You can't do anything, because I've got your magic coin. HA!"

He stuck out his tongue at her, touching his thumb to the tip of his crooked nose and wiggling his fingers.

"Take off those clothes right now and give Brianna back her endless coin," said Kirsty, putting her hands on her hips.

"It's wrong to take things that don't belong to you."

"You can't tell me what to do," said the goblin, sticking out his bottom lip. "You're not the boss of me. I'm on a special mission for Jack Frost!"

Buttons took a step toward the goblin and growled. He didn't like anyone shouting at Rachel or Kirsty. The goblin shrieked in terror and jumped back into the wardrobe.

"Get it away from me!" he wailed.

"I've been trapped in this tiny closet for hours. My neck hurts and my back hurts and I haven't found even one tooth for Jack Frost yet!"

"Give me back the endless coin and I'll use my magic to give you something for Jack Frost," said Brianna.

The goblin peered out of the wardrobe suspiciously.

"Really?" he asked.

"I promise," said Brianna.

The goblin grabbed one of Rachel's purses from inside the wardrobe and opened it. Then he held up the glimmering endless coin and dropped it into the purse.

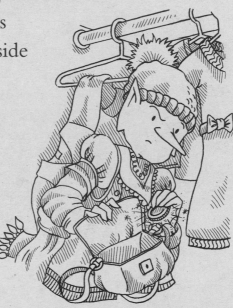

"Come and get it, then," he said.

As Brianna darted toward the purse, the girls saw the goblin smirk. What was he planning?

"No!" cried Rachel.

"It's a trap!" Kirsty shouted at the same instant. "Stop!"

They were both too late. Brianna
flew into the purse, and the goblin
snapped it shut with a cackle of
triumph. The Tooth Fairy was now his
prisoner!

Goblin on Wheels

"Why did you do that?" Rachel cried. "Brianna was offering to help you!"

"I don't want her help," the goblin said. "Yesterday she sent three goblins back to Jack Frost with some windup teeth that weren't even real. I'm not making the same mistake as they did! I'm too smart for you humans and fairies. You can't trick me!"

"Let her go right now," said Kirsty.

"No way," said the goblin. "I'm taking her to the Ice Castle with me. Jack Frost will keep her prisoner until she agrees to give him all the loose teeth she collects from children."

Buttons growled again, and the goblin trembled. That gave Rachel an idea. She put her hand on Buttons's collar.

"I'll take Buttons into the other room if you'll let Brianna go," she said.

The goblin nodded eagerly. Rachel opened the bedroom door and took Buttons into her parents' room. But as soon as the dog was out of sight, the goblin whooped and pushed past Kirsty. She fell back onto Rachel's bed. The goblin lunged over to Kirsty's bed, scooped up her tooth, and dashed out the door.

"Stop!" cried Kirsty furiously. "We had a deal!"

The goblin didn't reply. He ran down the stairs at top speed, clutching the purse with Brianna in it to his chest. Kirsty pulled herself up and ran out into the hallway, just in time to hear the front door slam shut.

"Rachel, come quickly!" she called. "He's getting away!"

Rachel dashed out of her parents' room. "We have to follow him!" she said. "We can't let him take Brianna to the Ice Castle. Come on!"

The girls raced downstairs, pulled on their shoes, and rushed outside. They peered up and down the street.

"He's already gone!" said Kirsty in alarm. "We're too late!"

"No, there he is!" Rachel cried, pointing to the far end of the street. "I just saw him duck down behind that big garbage can."

They sprinted up the street, and the goblin realized that he had been spotted. He started to run, too, but his thick layers of clothes slowed him down.

He had pulled Rachel's knitted hat down low over his ears and was clutching her purse tightly to his chest. He looked like an eccentric little old lady, and people turned around in surprise as he waddled past them. The sun was already shining brightly, making the goblin look very hot and uncomfortable.

"We're faster than he is," said Kirsty, panting. "We've almost caught him!"

The goblin looked over his shoulder and screeched in alarm. He ran up to a little boy playing with his scooter in the driveway of a house.

"Give me that!" he shouted, wrenching the scooter out of the boy's hands.

"That's mine!" wailed the little boy.

"Mine now!" sneered the goblin.

He jumped onto
the scooter and
disappeared
around the
corner at
top speed.
Kirsty and
Rachel
stopped
beside the
crying boy
and caught
their breath.

"That old lady took my scooter!" the
little boy sobbed.

"Don't cry," said Rachel, feeling very
sorry for him. "We'll try to get it back
for you."

Kirsty frowned. "How are we going to do that?" she wondered. "We're not fast enough to catch up to him."

Rachel and Kirsty looked at each other in dismay. What were they going to do now?

Four-Legged Hero

WOOF! WOOF!

There was a loud bark from behind the girls, and then Buttons raced past them. His ears streamed out behind him as he chased the goblin. He ran as fast as he could. In seconds, he had disappeared around the corner.

"Go, Buttons!" shouted Rachel. "Come on, Kirsty!"

Buttons knew that the girls wanted to catch the goblin. He was clearly determined to do his best to help them! They sprinted after him and ducked around the corner. They were just in time to see Buttons take a flying leap at the scooter! The goblin clattered to the pavement. He was so bundled up in Rachel's clothes that he bounced three times before rolling into

the gutter.
He lay there
on his back,
waving
his arms
and legs
helplessly
like a beetle.
He couldn't
get back onto his
feet! Buttons stood
next to him, panting with his mouth
hanging open.

"He looks just like he's laughing!" said
Kirsty as she stopped to catch her breath.
"Good boy, Buttons!"

The purse was lying on the pavement
next to the scooter. Rachel ran to open it
and Brianna flew out. She had her wand

in one hand, and the endless coin in the other. Brianna returned the coin to fairy-size and beamed from ear to ear.

"I knew you would rescue me!" she exclaimed.

"It wasn't us," said Rachel with a smile. "Buttons stopped the goblin and knocked him off the scooter."

Brianna gave Buttons a fairy kiss on the tip of his nose.

"Thank you, brave Buttons," she said. "You're my hero!"

Then she turned to the goblin and waved her wand at him. She said a quick spell.

"Stealing Rachel's clothes was wrong,
So send them back where they belong.
And give this dog a juicy bone
To have for a snack when he gets home."

The layers of clothes disappeared instantly, leaving the goblin dressed in his own short, ragged outfit. He growled and jumped to his feet, shaking his green fists at them all.

"I want that tooth!" he shouted. "I stole it fair and square!"

"This tooth belongs to Kirsty," said Brianna in a firm voice.

She placed the tooth in Kirsty's hand, and the goblin shrieked. Then Buttons growled, and the goblin's knees knocked together.

"I'm not waiting around for that monster to bite me!" he declared.

He ran off, and the girls sighed with relief.

"Thank goodness he's gone!" said Rachel.

"Can you take my tooth now that you have the endless coin back?" asked Kirsty hopefully.

Brianna's big smile faded slightly.

"I'm sorry," she said, "but I can't do anything with your tooth until I get the enchanted pouch back."

"We'll help you find it," said Rachel. "Where should we start?"

At that moment, the girls heard Mrs. Walker calling their names. Kirsty put her hand over her mouth.

"We just ran out without telling your mom where we were going!" she said to Rachel. "She must be worried about us."

"You should go home right away, and I should take the endless coin back to Fairyland," said Brianna. "But I'll be back as soon as I can, and then we can start our search for the enchanted pouch."

She waved her wand and disappeared in a flurry of golden sparkles. Kirsty picked up the fallen scooter, and Rachel patted Buttons. "Come on, boy, let's go home," she said. "Brianna promised that there would be a nice bone waiting for you!"

The girls and Buttons hurried back to Rachel's house. They stopped on the way to return the scooter to the little boy, whose tears dried at once.

Mrs. Walker was standing in the front yard, pruning a tree.

"Did Buttons run off?" she asked. "I thought it was strange that you didn't say where you were going!"

Rachel and Kirsty just smiled. She wouldn't believe the real story!

They went into the kitchen to finish their breakfast. Buttons discovered a large, juicy bone waiting for him in his bowl.

"What a great start to the day!" said Kirsty, pouring milk on her cornflakes.

"We helped Brianna find the endless coin, and it's not even nine o'clock yet!" said Rachel with a laugh. "I have a feeling that this is going to be a very good day!"

The Enchanted Pouch

Contents

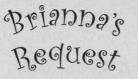

Brianna's Request

"Good shot!" Rachel exclaimed.
"You win!"

She picked up the badminton birdie
and grinned at Kirsty. They had been
playing badminton over an old tennis net
in the backyard all afternoon.

"Another game?" asked Kirsty. "We've

each won five now. This can be the
deciding match."

Mrs. Walker leaned out of the kitchen
window. "Would you girls like a drink?"
she called.

"In a minute,
Mom," Rachel
replied. "We're
going to play one
more game."

It was Kirsty's
turn to serve. She
held out the birdie,
aimed, and then
hit it with her
racquet. The birdie
flew higher . . .
and higher . . . and
higher!

"Wow!" said Rachel, looking up and shading her eyes from the sun. "That was an amazing shot!"

"I can't even see it," said Kirsty, peering into the clear blue sky. "I've never hit a shot like that before."

"There it is," said Rachel. "It's coming back down."

"I don't think that's the birdie," said Kirsty. "It's a different shape."

"You're right!" said Rachel in excitement. "It's Brianna!"

Brianna the Tooth Fairy swooped
down and perched on the top of the net.
She fluttered her wings slightly to keep
her balance.

"Hi, girls!" she
said with a
bright smile.
"I've come
to ask you
a big
favor."
Rachel
and Kirsty
dropped
their racquets
on the grass and
ran up to the net.

"It's great to see you, Brianna," said
Kirsty. "Have you found out where your

enchanted
pouch is?"

"Not
exactly," said
Brianna. "But
I've been
thinking
about what
the goblin said
this morning.
He wanted to
take me and

your loose tooth back to the Ice Castle.
I'm sure that Jack Frost must have the
enchanted pouch there with him."

"That makes sense," said Rachel. "The
enchanted pouch is where your Tooth
Fairy magic is kept. He must want to
keep it as safe as possible."

"Yes," Kirsty agreed. "He thinks it will stop his toothache. How can we help?"

"Will you come to the Ice Castle with me?" asked the little fairy. "I have to find my enchanted pouch, but Jack Frost's castle is a scary place. I know you've both been there before, so I thought you might know the best places to look."

"Of course we'll come," Rachel said immediately.

She looked up at the kitchen window. Her mom was inside, washing dishes. Rachel knew that they wouldn't be missed, because fairy magic would make time stand still in the human world while they were away.

"Let's go down to the edge of the yard," said Kirsty. "No one will be able to see us there."

As soon as they were out of sight, Brianna raised her wand. A stream of glittering fairy dust whooshed into the air. It curled around the girls like a golden ribbon.

They felt a warm glow as the fairy magic started to work. Gauzy wings appeared on their backs, and the world around them disappeared.

A few minutes later, the sparkles faded and they found themselves flying over a forest of snow-covered trees. Spiky towers glittering with ice rose up in the distance.

"Look, there's Jack Frost's castle," said Rachel. "We're almost there!"

A Toothache and a Teddy Bear

Rachel, Kirsty, and Brianna fluttered down to the edge of the forest. Their feet crunched on fresh snow as they landed.

"It's so cold!" said Brianna, rubbing her bare arms.

Rachel and Kirsty were already shivering. Brianna flicked her wand, and instantly, they were both snuggled into thick faux-fur jackets.

"That's better," said Kirsty. "Now, how are we going to get into the Ice Castle?"

They peered up at the towers of Jack Frost's chilling home. Goblin guards paced up and down, keeping watch.

"I've never seen so many guards here before," said Rachel. "Jack Frost must have something very important inside — something that he wants to protect."

"My enchanted pouch is definitely here," said Brianna, tightening her lips.

Kirsty gazed at the highest snowcapped tower and noticed a window being flung open.

"Up there!" she exclaimed. "Someone just opened a window. Come on — that's our way in!"

"What if one of the guards sees us?" asked Brianna.

"The goblins are usually too busy arguing with one another to pay much attention," said Rachel. "Besides, I think it's a chance we have to take."

Brianna nodded in agreement. The three friends rose up into the air and flew as fast as they could toward the highest tower. Blue curtains decorated with silver ice bolts billowed out of the open window. Rachel, Kirsty, and Brianna quietly landed on the window ledge and slipped inside.

They could hear voices and a high-pitched whining sound.

"I wonder where we are," said Rachel.

She peered around the side of the curtain and drew in her breath sharply.

She turned to Kirsty and Brianna and motioned them over.

"We're in Jack Frost's bedroom!" she whispered.

Kirsty and Brianna gasped and peeked around the side of the curtain. Jack Frost was sitting up in bed. A white cloth was wrapped under his chin and tied on the top of his head in a large bow. He clutched a spiky teddy bear and whimpered loudly.

"That's the teddy bear that Sabrina the Sweet Dreams Fairy gave him," said Kirsty. "What's wrong with him?" Rachel asked.

"He needs to have that tooth pulled," said Brianna. "Poor Jack Frost — he looks like he's in a lot of pain."

"I bet that hasn't made his temper any better," said Kirsty. "Look how the goblins are keeping their distance from him!"

At the farthest end
of the room from
the bed, three
goblins argued
in loud voices.
They all wore
white coats
that were too
big for them.

"Those are
dentists' coats,"
said Rachel. "I
bet they stole them from the dentist's
office."

"He needs a special potion," said the
first goblin. "I think we should make a
magic brew of weeds, mud, onion peel,
and moldy berries."

"That won't help a toothache," scoffed the second goblin. "That's for hiccups! He needs hot-water bottles strapped to his ears."

"Nonsense!" squawked the third goblin. "That tooth has gone bad. It needs to be pulled out."

"Yes!" said the first goblin. "How should we do that?"

"I know," said the second goblin. "We need to use his wand and take the tooth out with a magic thunderbolt!"

"No, no," the third goblin said, putting his hands on his hips. "We just have to tie a piece of string around his tooth. Then we pull it out by tying the other end to a door handle."

"That sounds like fun!" said the second goblin. "Let's try it!"

Uncle Jack Frost!

"I can't let them do this!" cried Brianna.

Before Rachel or Kirsty could stop her, she darted out from behind the curtain and fluttered into the center of the room to face the goblins.

"Stop!" she demanded. "I am the Tooth Fairy, and I can't let you go through with this terrible idea. You'll just make things even worse."

Jack Frost loosened the cloth around his head.

"It hurts so much!" he bellowed. He clutched his jaw and groaned. "It can't GET any worse!"

"A fairy!" yelled the goblins. "A fairy in Jack Frost's bedroom! Get her!"

"You need to go
to the dentist,"
said Brianna,
turning to Jack
Frost. "That's
the only way
you'll feel any
better."

"I'm not going to
let a silly dentist torture
me!" Jack Frost screeched.

Rachel and Kirsty flew out to join
their friend.

"You should listen to Brianna," Kirsty
said. "She knows a lot more about teeth
than these goblins."

"No she doesn't!" shouted the first
goblin. "She doesn't even have a
white coat!"

"Listen to me," said Brianna, flying over to Jack Frost and landing on the blanket in front of him. "A dentist won't hurt you. They take care of your teeth and make you feel better!"

Jack Frost stared at her. He was wincing in pain. "I'm scared," he said in a small voice. Rachel and Kirsty suddenly felt very sorry for him. They landed on the bed beside Brianna.

"Listen," said Rachel. "I've been going to Tippington Dental Care all of my life, and the dentist has never hurt me."

Jack Frost looked at her suspiciously.

"Really?" he asked.

"I love going there," Rachel continued. "They use a cool special dye that makes your teeth turn blue where you haven't brushed well enough."

"Yes, and they use toothpaste that tastes like bubblegum," Kirsty added.

"And they give you a 'good patient' sticker at the end," said Rachel.

"We could take you to the Tippington dentist

right now," said Brianna. "You could be feeling better in half an hour."

Jack Frost's eyes shone, and then he winced in pain.

"All right!" he said. "I'll go. But if they hurt me, I'll blame you!"

"Fine," said Brianna. "First, you need to look like an ordinary human."

She brushed her wand over Jack Frost's head like a hairbrush. His spikes smoothed down until they looked like hair, and his pajamas were replaced by a T-shirt and jeans.

Then Brianna waved her wand in the air. A flash of bright

golden light lit up the bedroom, and
Rachel and Kirsty closed their eyes.
When they opened them again, they
were hovering next to Brianna in an
alley, close to Tippington Dental Care.
Jack Frost stood in front of them, still
clutching his teddy bear.

"Are you ready to
go in?" Brianna
asked him.

Jack Frost
shook his head.
"I can't," he
wailed. "It's too
scary!"

"Brianna, I
have an idea,"
said Kirsty. "If
you turn us back

into humans, we can pretend to be
Jack Frost's nieces. Then we can go
in with him and help him feel more
brave."

Brianna waved her wand and returned
the girls to human-size. Kirsty and
Rachel each took one of Jack Frost's
arms. They marched him out of the

alley, up the steps of the dentist's office, and into the waiting room.

"Hello," said Rachel to the receptionist. "We need an emergency appointment, please. Our uncle has a terrible toothache!"

A Brave Patient

Jack Frost was very nervous. He paced up and down in the waiting room, squeezing his teddy bear. Luckily, they didn't have to wait very long. The door to the exam room opened, and the dentist looked out.

"Mr. Frost?" she asked.

Jack Frost didn't move, but Rachel and Kirsty took his arms and led him gently into the exam room. The dentist raised her eyebrows. She raised them even higher when she saw the spiky teddy bear, but she didn't say anything about it.

"Let's see if I can help you feel better today, Mr. Frost," she said with a warm smile.

She guided him into the chair. There was a sailboat mobile dangling from the ceiling, with red and blue boats swirling slowly around.

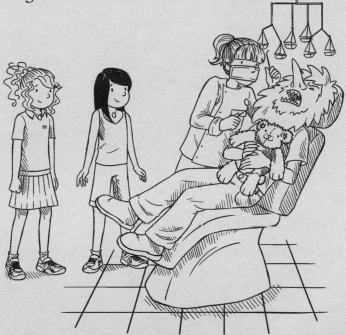

"Just lean back, look at the mobile, and try to relax," said the dentist. "Open wide."

"Is it all right if we stay?" asked Kirsty. "Our uncle is a little nervous."

"Of course," the dentist replied, peering into Jack Frost's mouth. "Goodness, what spiky teeth you have, Mr. Frost! But I see the problem tooth. I can fix that right up for you."

It was all over very quickly. The dentist pulled out the bad tooth and gave Jack Frost some blue liquid to rinse out his mouth. Then she dropped the tooth into his hand.

"There you are," she said with a smile. "How do you feel now?"

"The pain's completely gone!" said Jack Frost. "I was very brave, wasn't I?"

The dentist hid a smile. "Yes, you were very brave," she agreed.

"Where's my 'good patient' sticker?" Jack Frost demanded.

"They're usually just for our younger patients. . . ." the dentist began.

"I AM young!" roared Jack Frost.

"He's back to his normal self already," Rachel whispered in Kirsty's ear.

The dentist gave Jack Frost a large "good patient" sticker, and he stuck it proudly on his T-shirt.

"One for Teddy, too," he snapped.

The dentist gave the teddy bear a sticker, too. Then she handed Jack Frost a little bag.

"There is a toothbrush, a tube of toothpaste, and some mouthwash in there," she said. "I would like you to brush your teeth twice a day from now on and eat less sugar. I don't want to have to pull out any more of your teeth, Mr. Frost!"

"Thank you very much," said Rachel, realizing that Jack Frost wasn't going to be polite enough to say it.

The dentist
opened the
door and
followed them
out into the
waiting room.

"Has my next
patient arrived?"
she asked the receptionist.

"No," the receptionist replied. "That's
the third person who hasn't showed up
today. You've gotten three more calls
from patients you saw this morning,
saying that their teeth have been
hurting."

The dentist groaned, and Kirsty and
Rachel looked at each other. They
followed Jack Frost out of the dentist's
office and down the steps.

"Things are going wrong for the dentist because you still have the enchanted pouch," Kirsty said to him.

"It's really unfair of you to keep it after the dentist and Brianna helped you so much today." Jack Frost was only half listening. He held up his tooth so that it gleamed in the sunshine, and gazed at it lovingly.

"Isn't it wonderful?" he said. "Nice and spiky! I'd much rather have this tooth than some pesky fairy's silly pouch."

"Do you mean that?" asked Rachel in an eager voice.

This might be their chance to get Brianna's enchanted pouch back!

The Magic
of the Pouch

The girls pulled Jack Frost into the alley where Brianna was waiting for them. He narrowed his eyes.

"If I give back the pouch, what do I get out of it?" he asked.

Rachel and Kirsty groaned. He was back to his old mean self. But Brianna smiled at him.

"That's a wonderful tooth," she said. "It's one of the best I've ever seen."

Flattered, Jack Frost gave a smug little smile. "If I had my enchanted pouch back, I could make you an icy display stand for the tooth," Brianna continued. "But I would need to use the special magic that's in the enchanted pouch."

Jack Frost reached into his pocket and pulled out a small velvet pouch. It glowed as he held it out to Brianna.

"Take it," he said. "I want a display stand!"

Brianna took the pouch and shrank it to fairy-size with her wand. She pulled on the gold braid that held the pouch closed and took a pinch of fairy dust from inside. Then she recited the words of a spell.

"Tooth magic old and tooth magic new,
Use your power strong and true.
Give this tooth a place to sit
Where icy light can shine on it."

Brianna threw the fairy dust up, and it drew itself together, making a shape in midair. The shape grew more solid and formed an amazing display stand, which landed on the ground in front of Jack Frost. It was a miniature version of his Ice Castle, complete with towers and icicles. On the central tower sat a tiny, blue velvet cushion. Jack Frost gasped with delight and placed his tooth on the cushion.

"I think he likes it," said Kirsty with a laugh.

Jack Frost pulled his wand from inside his T-shirt and tapped himself on the head. His hair sprang up into its usual spikes, and his blue cloak replaced his human clothes. Without even glancing at Rachel, Kirsty, and Brianna, he flourished his wand. With a loud thunderclap and a rush of icy wind, Jack Frost disappeared, taking along his tooth, his teddy bear, and his display stand.

Brianna sighed with relief.

"He's gone back to his Ice Castle, thank goodness!" she said. "You were both terrific! I couldn't have gotten my pouch back without you."

"We enjoyed it," said Kirsty with a laugh. "I'll never forget seeing Jack Frost get a 'good patient' sticker!"

"Thank you for everything," said Brianna. "It's time for me to go back to Fairyland, so good-bye — for now!" She winked at them and then vanished in a puff of fairy dust. Rachel and Kirsty smiled at each other. They would never forget today, either!

That night, Kirsty went to sleep with her tooth under her pillow. When she woke up in the morning, she slipped her hand under her pillow and felt something that hadn't been there the night before. Kirsty drew her hand out slowly.

"What did Brianna leave for you?" asked Rachel, bounding over to her bed.

Kirsty opened her hand, and the girls saw two objects lying there. One was a shiny dollar coin. The other was a narrow silver ring, set with a tiny shimmering stone.

"Is it a pearl?" asked Kirsty, holding it up to the light.

The stone had transparent walls, and something inside was sparkling.

"No, it's not a pearl," said Rachel in excitement. "I know what it is! Brianna has given you a moonstone that looks like your tooth!"

The girls shared a smile.

"This adventure has been a lot of fun," said Kirsty. "Now I'm really, really looking forward to losing my next tooth!"

SPECIAL EDITION

Don't miss Rachel and Kirsty's
other fairy adventures!
Join them as they try to help

Belle
the Birthday Fairy!

Read on for a special sneak peek. . . .

Parties in Peril!

"I can't wait to see Mom's face when she arrives at her surprise birthday party!" Rachel Walker said with a little skip of excitement.

"Yes, she'll be so amazed when she realizes that you and your dad arranged it all!" replied her best friend, Kirsty Tate, swinging her rollerskates happily.

Kirsty was staying at Rachel's house in Tippington during school break. Rachel's mom thought that Kirsty was just there for a visit, but she was also there to attend Mrs. Walker's surprise party!

"Everything's ready," said Rachel, counting things off on her fingers. "The food, the music, the decorations for the village hall . . ."

"What about the cake?" Kirsty asked.

"Dad ordered that from the bakery," said Rachel with a smile. "He's not very good at baking, and he wanted it to be perfect!"

The friends were on their way to the local park to go rollerskating. As they passed the village hall where Mrs. Walker's party was going to be, Rachel squeezed Kirsty's hand.

"Let's just quickly look inside," she said. "I want to show you where I'm planning to put all the decorations on the day of the party."

"Ooh, yes!" said Kirsty eagerly. "I can't wait to help you decorate the hall and lay out the food."

They peeked in the door — and their mouths fell open in astonishment. A group of boys and girls were there in their best party outfits, but no one seemed to be having a good time. The guests were talking in low voices. They all looked upset! Some of the parents were kneeling on the floor, cleaning up squished cakes and spilled drinks. A box of decorations sat untouched by the window. There was a stereo on the stage, but it was making a strange whining sound and there was smoke coming out of the top.

A little girl was standing by the door with her head down. She was wearing a pretty pink dress with a white sash, but she looked very sad.

"Hello," said Rachel. "Is this your party?"

The little girl nodded her head. Her big blue eyes filled with tears.

RAINBOW magic™

There's Magic in Every Series!

The Rainbow Fairies
The Weather Fairies
The Jewel Fairies
The Pet Fairies
The Fun Day Fairies
The Petal Fairies
The Dance Fairies
The Music Fairies
The Sports Fairies
The Party Fairies
The Ocean Fairies
The Night Fairies
The Magical Animal Fairies
The Princess Fairies
The Superstar Fairies

Read them all!

■ SCHOLASTIC

scholastic.com
rainbowmagiconline.com

HIT entertainment

RMFAIRY